J. Cole

Emma Gellibrand

Contents

J. COLE

BY

Emma Gellibrand

J. COLE.

"HONNERD MADAM,

"Wich i hav seed in the paper a page Boy wanted, and begs to say J. Cole is over thertene, and I can clene plate, wich my brutther is under a butler and lernd me, and I can wate, and no how to clene winders and boots. J. Cole opes you will let me cum. I arsks 8 and all found. if you do my washin I will take sevven. J. Cole will serve you well and opes to giv sattisfaxshun. i can cum tomorrer.J. COLE.

"P.S.--He is not verry torl but growin. My brutther is a verry good hite. i am sharp and can rede and rite and can hadd figgers if you like."

CHAPTER I.

I had advertised for a page-boy, and having puzzled through some dozens of answers, more or less illegible and impossible to understand, had come to the last one of the packet, of which the above is an exact copy.

The epistle was enclosed in a clumsy envelope, evidently home-made, with the aid of scissors and gum, and was written on a half-sheet of letter-paper, in a large hand, with many blots and smears, on pencilled lines.

There was something quaint and straightforward in the letter, in spite of the utter ignorance of grammar and spelling; and while I smiled at the evident pride in the "brutther" who was a "verry good hite," and the offer to take less wages if "I would do his washin," I found myself wondering what sort of waif upon the sea of life was this not very tall person, over thirteen, who "would serve me well."

I had many letters to answer and several appointments to make, and had scarcely made up my mind whether or not to trouble to write to my accomplished correspondent, who was "sharp, and could rede and rite, and hadd figgers," when, a shadow falling on the ground by me as I sat by the open window, I looked up, and saw, standing opposite my chair, a boy,--the very smallest boy, with the very largest blue eyes I ever saw. The clothes on his little limbs were evidently meant for somebody almost double his size, but they were clean and tidy.

In one hand he held a bundle, tied in a red handkerchief, and in the other a bunch of wild-flowers that bore signs of having travelled far in the heat of the sun, their blossoms hanging down, dusty and fading, and their petals dropping one by one on the ground.

"Who are you, my child?" I said, "and what do you want?"

At my question the boy placed his flowers on my table, and, pulling off his cap, made a queer movement with his feet, as though he were trying to step backwards with both at once, and said, in a voice so deep that it quite startled me, so strangely did it seem to belong to the size of the clothes, and not the wearer,--

"Please'm, it's J. Cole; and I've come to live with yer. I've brought all my clothes, and every think."

For the moment I felt a little bewildered, so impossible did it seem that the small specimen of humanity before me was actually intending to enter anybody's service; he looked so childish and wistful, and yet with a certain honesty of purpose shining out of those big, wide- open eyes, that interested me in him, and made me want to know more of him.

"You are very small to go into service," I said, "and I am afraid you could not do the work I should require; besides, you should have waited to hear from me, and then have come to see me, if I wanted you to do so."

"Yes, I know I'm not very big," said the boy, nervously fidgeting with his bundle; "leastways not in hite; but my arms is that long, they'll reach ever so 'igh above my 'ed, and as for bein' strong, you should jest see me lift my father's big market basket when it's loaded with 'taters, or wotever is for market, and I hope you'll not be angry because I come to-day; but Dick--that's my brutther Dick--he says, 'You foller my advice, Joe,' he says, 'and go arter this 'ere place, and don't let no grass grow under your feet. I knows what it is goin' arter places; there's such lots a fitin' after 'em, that if you lets so much as a hour go afore yer looks 'em up, there's them as slips in fust gets it; and wen yer goes to the door they opens it and sez, "It ain't no use, boy, we're sooted;" and then where are yer, I'd like to know? So,' sez he, 'Joe, you look sharp and go, and maybe you'll get it.' So I come, mum, and please, that's all."

"But about your character, my boy," I said. "You must have somebody to speak for you, and say you are honest, and what you are able to do. I always want a good character with my servants; the last page- boy I had brought three years' good character from his former situation."

"Lor!" said Joe, with a serious look, "did he stay three years in a place afore he came to you? Wotever did he leave them people for, where he were so comfortable? If I stay with you three years, you won't catch me a leavin' yer, and goin' somewheres else. Wot a muff that chap was!"

I explained that it did not always depend on whether a servant wanted to stay or not, but whether it suited the employers to keep him.

"'Praps he did somethin', and they giv' 'im the sack," murmured Joe; "he was a flat!"

"But about this character of yours," I said; "if I decide to give you a trial, although I am almost sure you are too small, and won't do, where am I to go for your character? Will the people where your brother lives speak for you?"

"Oh, yes!" cried the little fellow, his cheeks flushing; "I know Dick'll ask 'em to give me a caricter. Miss Edith, I often cleaned 'er boots. Once she come 'ome in the mud, and was a-goin' out agin directly; and they was lace-ups, and a orful bother to do up even; and she come into the stable-yard with 'er dog, and sez: 'Dick, will you chain Tiger up, and this little boy may clean my boots if he likes, on my feet?' So I cleaned 'em, and she giv' me sixpence; and after that, when the boots come down in the mornin', I got Dick always to let me clean them little boots, and I kep 'em clean in the insides, like the lady's maid she told me not to put my 'ands inside 'em if they was black. Miss Edith, she'll giv me a caricter, if Dick asks 'er."

Just then the visitors' bell rang; and I sent my would-be page into the kitchen to wait until I could speak to him again, and told him to ask the cook to give him something to eat.

"Here are your flowers," I said; "take them with you."

He looked at me, and then, as if ashamed of having offered them, gathered them up in his hands, and with the corner of the red handkerchief wiped some few leaves and dust-marks off my table, then saying in a low voice, "I didn't know you 'ad beauties of yer own, like them in the glass pots, but I'll giv' 'em to the cook." So saying, he went away into the kitchen, and my visitors came in, and by and by some more friends arrived.

The weather was very warm, and we sat chattering and enjoying the shade of the trees by the open French window. Presently, somebody being thirsty, I suggested lemonade and ice, and I offered strawberries, and (if possible) cream; though my mind misgave me as to the latter delicacy, for we had several times been obliged to do without some of our luxuries if they entailed "fetching," as we had no boy to run errands quickly on an emergency and be useful. However, I rang the bell; and when the housemaid, whose temper, since she had been what is curiously termed in servants'-hall language "single- handed," was most trying, entered, I said, "Make some lemonade, Mary, and ask cook to gather some strawberries quickly, and bring them, with some cream."

Mary looked at me as who should say, "Well, I'm sure! and who's to do it all? You'll have to wait a bit." And I know we should have to wait, and therefore resigned myself to do so patiently, keeping up the ball of gossip, and wondering if a little music later on would perhaps while away the time.

Much to my amazement, in less than a quarter of an hour Mary entered with the tray, all being prepared; and directly I looked at the strawberry-bowl I detected a novel feature in the table decoration. A practised hand had evidently been at work; but whose? Mary was far too matter-of-fact a person. Food, plates, knives and forks, glasses, and a cruet-stand were all she ever thought necessary; and even for a centre vase of flowers I had to ask, and often to insist, during the time she was single-handed.

But here was my strawberry-bowl, a pretty one, even when unadorned, with its pure white porcelain stem, intwined with a wreath of blue convolvulus, and then a spray of white, the petals just peeping over the edge of the bowl, and resting near the luscious red fruit; the cream-jug, also white, had twining flowers of blue, and round the lemonade-jug, of glass, was a wreath of yellow blossoms.

"How exquisite!" exclaimed we all. "What fairy could have bestowed such a treat to our eyes and delight to our sense of the beautiful?"

I supposed some friend of the cook's or Mary's had been taking lessons in the art of decoration, and had given us a specimen.

Soon after, my friends having gone, I thought of J. Cole waiting to be dismissed, and sent for him.

Cook came in, and with a preliminary "Ahem!" which I knew of old meant, "I have an idea of my own, and I mean to get it carried out," said, "Oh, if you please 'm, if I might be so bold, did you think serious of engagin' the boy that's waitin' in the kitchen?"

"Why do you ask, Cook? "I said.

"Well, ma'am," she replied, trying to hide a laugh, "of course it's not for me to presume; but, if I might say a word for him, I think he's the very handiest and the sharpest one we've ever had in this house, and we've had a many, as you know. Why, if you'd only have seen him when Mary come in in her tantrums at 'aving to get the tray single-handed, and begun a-grumblin' and a-bangin' things about, as is her way, being of a quick temper, though, as I tells her, too slow a-movin' of herself. As I were a-sayin', you should have seen that boy. If he didn't up and leave his bread and butter and mug of milk, as he was a-enjoyin' of as 'arty as you like, and, 'Look 'ere,' says he, 'giv' me the jug. I'll make some fine drink with lemons. I see Dick do it often up at his place. Giv' me the squeezer. Wait till I washes my 'ands. I won't be a minnit.' Then in he rushes into the scullery, washes his hands, runs back again in a jiffy. 'Got any snow sugar? I mean all done fine like snow.' I gave it him; and, sure enough, his little hands moved that quick, he had made the lemonade before Mary would have squeezed a lemon. 'Where do yer buy the cream?' he says next. 'I'll run and get it while you picks the strawberries.' Perhaps it wasn't right, me a trustin' him, being a stranger, but he was that quick I couldn't say no. Up he takes the jug, and was off; and when I come in from the garden with the strawberries, if he hadn't been and put all them flowers on the things. He begs my pardon for interfering like, and says, 'I 'ope you'll excuse me a-doin' of it, but the woman at the milk-shop said I might 'ave 'em; and I see the butler where Dick lives wind the flowers about like that, and 'ave 'elped 'im often; and, please, I paid for the cream, because I'd got two bob of my own, Dick giv' me on my birthday. Oh, I do 'ope, Mrs. Cook,' he says, 'that the lady'll take me; I 'll serve 'er well, I will, indeed;' and then he begins to cry and tremble, poor little chap, for he'd been running about a lot, and never eaten or drank what I gave him, because he wanted to help, and it was hot in the kitchen, I suppose, and he felt faint like, but there he is, crying; and just now, when the bell rung, which was two great big boys after the place, he says, 'Oh, please say "We're sooted," and ask the lady if I may stay.' So, I've taken the liberty, ma'am," said Cook, "for somehow I like that little chap, and there's a deal in him, I do believe."

So saying, Cook retired; and, in a moment, J. Cole was standing in her place, the blue eyes brimming over with tears, and an eager anxiety as to what his fate would be making his poor little hands clutch at his coat-sleeves, and his feet shuffle about so nervously, that I had not the courage to grieve him by a refusal.

"Well, Joseph," I said, "I have decided to give you a month's trial. I shall write to the gentleman who employs your brother; and if he speaks well of you, you may stay."

"And may I stay now, please?" he said. "May I stay before you gets any answer to your letter to say I'm all right? I think you'd better let me; there ain't no boy; and Mrs. Cook and Mary'll 'ave a lot to do. I can stay in the stable, if you don't like to let me be in the house, afore you writes the letter."

"No, Joe," I replied: "you may not be a good, honest boy, but I think you are; and you shall stay here. Now go back to Mrs. Wilson, and finish your milk, and eat something more if you can, then have a good rest and a wash; they will show you where you are to sleep, and at dinner, this evening, I shall see if you can wait at table."

"Thank you very kindly," said the boy, his whole face beaming with delight, "and I'll be sure and do everythink I can for you." Then he went quickly out of the room; for I could see he was quite overcome, now that the uncertainty was over.

Alone once more, I reasoned with myself, and felt I was doing an unwise thing. Just at that time my husband was away on business for some months; and I had no one to advise me, and no one to say me nay either. My conscience told me my husband would say, "We cannot tell who this boy is, where he has lived, or who are his associates; he may be connected with a gang of thieves for what we know to the contrary. Wait, and have proper references before trusting him in the house."

And he would be right to say so to me, but not every one listens to conscience when it points the opposite way to inclination. Well, J. Cole remained; and when I entered the dining-room, to my solitary dinner, he was there, with a face shining from soap and water, his curls evidently soaped too, to make them go tidily on his forehead. The former page having left his livery jacket and trousers, Mary had let Joe dress in them, at his earnest request.

She told me afterwards that he had sewn up the clothes in the neatest manner wherever they could be made smaller; and the effect of the jacket, which he had stuffed out in the chest with hay, as we discovered by the perfume, was very droll. He had a great love of bright colors, and the trousers being large, showed bright red socks; the jacket sleeves being much too short for the long arms, of which he was so proud, allowed the wristbands of a vivid blue flannel shirt to be seen.

I was alone, so could put up with this droll figure at my elbow; but the seriousness of his face was such a contrast to the comicality of the rest of him, that I found myself beginning to smile every now and then, but directly I saw the serious eyes on me, I felt obliged to become grave at once.

The waiting at table I could not exactly pronounce a success; for, although Joe's quick eyes detected in an instant if I wanted anything, his anxiety to be "first in the field," and give Mary no chance of instructing him in his duties, made him collide against her more than once in his hasty rushes to the sideboard and back to my elbow with the dishes, which he generally handed to me long before he reached me, his long arms enabling him to reach me with his hands while he was yet some distance from me, and often on the wrong side. I also noticed when I wanted water he lifted the water-bottle on high, and poured as though it was something requiring a "head." Mary nearly caused a catastrophe at that moment by frowning at him, and saying, sotto voce, "Whatever are you doing? Is that the way to pour out water? It ain't hale, stoopid!"

Joe's face became scarlet; and to hide his confusion he seized a dish-cover, and hastily went out of the room with it, returning in a moment pale and serious as became one who at heart was every inch a family butler with immense responsibilities.

Joe was quiet and sharp, quick and intelligent; but I could see he was quite new to waiting at table. To remove a dish was, I could see, his greatest dread; and it amused me to see the cleverness with which he managed that Mary should do that part of the duty.

When only my plate and a dish remained to be cleared away, he would slowly get nearer as I got towards the last morsel, and before Mary had time, would take my plate, and go quite slowly to the sideboard with it, leisurely remove the knife and fork, watching meanwhile in the mirror if Mary was about to take the dish away; if not he would take something outside, or bring a decanter, and ask if I wanted wine.

I was, however, pleased to find him no more awkward, as I feared he would have been, and when, having swept the grate and placed my solitary wineglass and dessert-plate on the table, he retired, softly closing the door after him, I felt I should make something of J. Cole, and hoped his character would be good.

CHAPTER II.

The next morning a tastefully arranged vase of flowers in the centre of the breakfast-table, and one magnificent rose and bud by my plate, were silent but eloquent appeals to my interest on behalf of my would-be page; and when Joe himself appeared, fresh from an hour's self-imposed work in my garden, I saw he had become quite one of the family; for Bogie, my little terrier, usually very snappish to strangers, and who considered all boys as his natural enemies, was leaping about his feet, evidently asking for more games, and our old magpie was perched familiarly on his shoulder.

"Good-morning, Joe," I said. "You are an early riser, I can see, by the work you have already done in the garden."

"Why, yes," replied Joe, blushing, and touching an imaginary cap; "I'm used to bein' up. There was ever so much to do of a mornin' at 'ome; and I 'ad to 'elp father afore I could go to be with Dick, and I was with Dick a'most every mornin' by seven, and a good mile and a arf to walk to 'is place. Shall I bring in the breakfust, mum? Mary's told me what to do."

Having given permission, Joe set to work to get through his duties, this time without any help, and I actually trembled when I saw him enter with a tray containing all things necessary for my morning meal, he looked so over-weighted; but he was quite equal to it as far as landing the tray safely on the sideboard. But, alas! then came the ordeal; not one thing did poor Joe know where to place, and stood with the coffeepot in his hand, undecided whether it went before me, or at the end of the table, or whether he was to pour out my coffee for me.

I saw he was getting very nervous, so took it from him, and in order to put him at his ease, I remarked,--

"I think, perhaps, I had better show you, Joe, just for once, how I like my breakfast served, for every one has little ways of their own, you know; and you will try to do it my way when you know how I like it, won't you?"

Thereupon I arranged the dishes, etc., for him, and his big eyes followed my every movement. The blinds wanted pulling down a little presently, and then I began to realize one of the drawbacks in having such a very small boy as page. Joe saw the sun's rays were nearly blinding me, and wanted to shut them out; but on attempting to reach the tassel attached to the cord, it was hopelessly beyond his reach. In vain were the long arms stretched to their utmost, till the sleeves of the ex-page's jacket retreated almost to Joe's elbows, but no use.

I watched, curious to see what he would do.

"Please 'm, might I fetch an 'all chair?" said Joe; "I'm afraid I'm not big enuf to reach the tossle, but I won't pull 'em up so 'igh to- morrow."

I gave permission, and carefully the chair was steered among my tables and china pots. Then Joe mounted, and by means of rising on the tips of his toes he was able to accomplish the task of lowering the blinds.

I noticed at that time that Joe wore bright red socks, and I little thought what a shock those bright-colored hose were to give me later on under different circumstances.

That evening I had satisfactory letters regarding Joe's character, and by degrees he became used to his new home, and we to him. His quaint sayings and wonderful love of the truth, added to extreme cleanliness, made him welcome in the somewhat exclusive circle in which my housekeeper, Mrs. Wilson, reigned supreme.

Many a hearty burst of laughter came to me from the open kitchen- window across the garden in the leisure hour, when, the servants' tea being over, they sat at work, while Joe amused them with his stories and reminiscences of the sayings and doings of his wonderful brother Dick.

This same Dick was evidently the one being Joe worshipped on earth, and to keep his promises to Dick was a sacred duty.

"You don't know our Dick, Mrs. Wilson," said Joe, to the old housekeeper; "if you did, you'd understand why I no more dare go agen wot Dick told me, than I dare put my 'and in that 'ere fire. When I were quite a little chap, I took some big yaller plums once, out of one of the punnits father was a-packin' for market, and I eat 'em. I don't know to this hour wot made me take them plums; but I remember they were such prime big uns, big as eggs they was, and like lumps of gold, with a sort of blue shade over 'em. Father were very partikler about not 'avin' the fruit 'andled and takin' the bloom off, and told me to cover 'em well with leaves. It was a broilin' 'ot day, and I was tired, 'avin' been stoopin' over the baskits since four in the morning, and as I put the leaves over the plums I touched 'em; they felt so lovely and cool, and looked so juicy-like, I felt I must eat one, and I did; there was just six on 'em, and when I'd bin and eat one, there seemed such a empty place left in the punnit, that I knew father'd be sure to see it, so I eat 'em all, and then threw the punnit to one side. Just then, father comes up and says, "Count them punnits, Dick! there ought to be forty on 'em. Twenty picked large for Mr. Moses, and twenty usuals for Marts!'--two of our best customers they was. Well, Dick, he counts 'em, and soon misses one. 'Thirty-eight, thirty-nine,' he sez, and no more; 'but 'ere's a empty punnit,' he sez. I was standing near, feelin' awful, and wished I'd said I'd eat the plums afore Dick begun to count 'em, but I didn't, and after that I couldn't. 'Joe!' sez Dick, 'I wants yer! 'Ow come this empty punnit 'ere, along of the others? there's plums bin in it, I can see, 'cos it's not new. Speak up, youngster!' I looked at Dick's face, Mrs. Wilson, and his eyes seemed to go right into my throat, and draw the truth out of me. 'Speak up,' he sez, a-gettin' cross; 'if you've prigged 'em, say so, and you'll get a good hidin' from me, for a-doin' of it; but if you tells me a lie, you'll get such a hidin' for that as 'll make you remember it all your life; so speak up, say you did it, and take your hidin' like a brick, and if you didn't prig 'em, say who did, 'cos you must 'av' seen 'em go.'

"I couldn't do nothin', Mrs. Wilson, but keep my 'ed down, and blubber out, 'Please, Dick, I eat 'em.'

"'Oh, you did, yer young greedy, did yer,' he sez; 'I'm glad yer didn't tell me a lie. I've got to giv' yer a hidin', Joe; but giv' us yer 'and, old chap, first, and mind wot I sez to yer: "Own up to it, wotever you do," and take your punishment; it's 'ard to bear, but when the smart on it's over yer forgets it; but if yer tells a lie to save yerself, yer feels the smart of *that* always; yer feels ashamed of yerself whenever yer thinks of it.' And then Dick give me a thrashin', he did, but I never 'ollered or made a row, tho' he hit pretty 'ard. And, Mrs. Wilson, I never could look in Dick's face if I told a lie, and I never shall tell one, I 'ope, as long as ever I live. You should just see Dick, Mrs. Wilson, he is a one-er, he is."

"Lor' bless the boy," said Mary, the housemaid; "why, if he isn't a- cryin' now. Whatever's the matter? One minnit you're makin' us larf fit to kill ourselves, and then you're nearly makin' us cry with your Dick, and your great eyes runnin' over like that. Now get away, and take the dogs their supper, and see if you can't get a bit of color in your cheeks before you come back."

So off Joe went, and soon the frantic barking in the stable-yard showed he had begun feeding his four-footed pets.

Time went on; it was a very quiet household just then--my husband away in America, and my friends most of them enjoying their summer abroad, or at some seaside place--all scattered here and there until autumn was over, and then we were to move to town, and spend the winter season at our house there. I hoped my dear sister and her girls would then join us, and, best of all, my dear husband be home to make our circle complete.

Day by day Joe progressed in favor with everybody; his size was always a trouble, but his extreme good nature made everybody willing to help him over his difficulties. He invented all sorts of curious tools for reaching up to high places; and the marvels he would perform with a long stick and a sort of claw at the end of it were quite astonishing.

I noticed whenever I spoke of going to town Joe did not seem to look forward to the change with any pleasure, although he had never been to London, he told me; but Dick had been once with his father, and had seen lots of strange things; among others a sad one, that made a great impression on Dick, and he had told the tale to Joe, so as to have almost as great an effect on him.

It appeared that one night Dick and his father were crossing Waterloo Bridge, and had seen a young girl running quickly along, crying bitterly. Dick tried to keep up with her, and asked her what was the matter. She told him to let her alone, that she meant to drown herself, for she had nothing to live for, and was sick of her life. Dick persuaded her to tell him her grief, and heard from her that her mother and father had both been drowned in a steamer, and she was left with a little brother to take care of; he had been a great trouble to her, and had been led away by bad companions until he became thoroughly wicked. She had been a milliner, and had a room of her own, and paid extra for a little place where her brother could sleep. She fed and clothed him out of her earnings, although he was idle, and cruel enough to scold and abuse her when she tried to reason with him, and refused to let him bring his bad companions to her home. At last he stole nearly all she had, and pawned it; and among other things, some bonnets and caps belonging to the people who employed her, given as patterns for her to copy. These she had to pay for, and lost her situation besides. By degrees all her clothes, her home, and all she had, went for food; and then this wicked boy left her, and the next thing she knew was that he had been taken up with a gang of burglars concerned in a jewel robbery. That day she had seen him in prison, and he was to be transported for seven years; so the poor creature, mad with grief, was about to end her life. Dick and his father would not leave her until she was quiet, and promised them she would go and get a bed and supper with the money they gave her, and they promised to see her again the next day at a place she named. The next morning they went to the address, and found a crowd round the house. Somebody said a young woman had thrown herself out of a window, and had been taken up dead. It was too true; and the girl was the wretched, heart-broken sister they had helped over night. Her grief had been too much for her, and, poor thing, she awoke to the light of another day, and could not face it alone and destitute; so, despairing, she had ended her life. They went to the hospital, and were allowed to see all that remained of the poor creature; and Dick's description of it all, and his opinion that the brother "might have been just such another little chap at first as Joe," and "What would that brother feel," said Dick, "when he knew what he had done? for he done it," said Dick; "he done that girl to death, the same as if he'd shov'd her out of that winder hisself."

"And," said Joe, "I wonder if them chaps is goin' about London now wot led her brother wrong? I don't like London; and I wish we could stop 'ere."

I assured Joe that in London there was no danger of meeting such people if he kept to himself, and made no friends of strangers.

Joe was also much afraid of having to wait at table when there were guests. In spite of all I could do, he was hopelessly nervous and confused when he had to wait on more than two or three people; and as I expected to entertain a good deal when we were in town, I could not help fearing Joe would be unequal to the duties.

I could not bear the idea of parting with the little fellow, for, added to his good disposition, Joe, in his dark brown livery, with gilt buttons, his neat little ties, and clean hands; his carefully brushed curls, by this time trained into better order, and shining like burnished gold in the sun; his tiny feet, with the favorite red socks, which he could and did darn very neatly himself when they began to wear out (and when he bought new ones they were always bright red),--Joe, let me tell you, was quite an ornament in our establishment, and the envy of several boys living in families round about, who tried in vain to get acquainted with him, but he would not be friends, although he always refused their advances with civil words.

Sometimes a boy would linger when bringing a note or message for me, and try to draw Joe into conversation. In a few minutes I would hear Joe's deep voice say, "I think you had better go on now. I've got my work to do, and I reckon you've got yours a-waiting for yer at your place." Then the side-door would shut, and Joe was bustling about his work.

CHAPTER III.

In the beginning of October we arrived in London. There had been much packing up, and much extra work for everybody, and Joe was in his element.

What those long arms, and that willing heart, and those quick little hands got through, nobody but those he helped and worked for could tell. Whatever was wanted Joe knew where to find it. Joe's knife was ready to cut a stubborn knot; Joe's shoulders ready to be loaded with as heavy a weight as any man could carry. More than once I met him coming down-stairs with large boxes he himself could almost have been packed in, and he declared he did not find them too heavy.

"You see, Missis," he said, "I'm that strong now since I've been here, with all the good food I gets, and bein' so happy like, that I feel almost up to carryin' anythink. I do believe I could lift that there pianner, if somebody would just give it a hoist, and let me get hold of it easy."

Yes, Joe was strong and well, and I am sure, happy, and I had never had a single misgiving about him since he stood with his fading flowers and shabby clothes at my window that summer day.

At last we were settled in town, and the winter season beginning. Our house was situated in the West End of London, a little beyond Bayswater. One of a row of detached houses, facing another row exactly similar in every way, except that the backs of those we lived in had small gardens, with each its own stable wall at the end, with coachman's rooms above, the front of the stable facing the mews, and having the entrance from there; the mews ran all along the backs of these houses. On the opposite side the houses facing ours had their gardens and back windows facing the high-road, and no stables. There was a private road belonging to this, Holling Park as it was called, and a watchman to keep intruders out, and to stop organ-grinders, beggars, and such invaders of the peace from disturbing us.

Somehow I was never as comfortable as in my snug cottage in the country. Rich, fashionable people lived about us, and all day long kept up the round of "society life."

In the morning the large handsome houses would seem asleep, nothing moving inside or out, except a tradesman's cart, calling for orders, or workmen putting up or taking down awnings, at some house where there would be, or had been, a ball or entertainment of some kind. About eleven a carriage or two would be driven round from the mews, and stop before a house to take some one for a morning drive; but very seldom was anybody on foot seen about. In the afternoon it was different,-- carriages rolled along incessantly, and streams of afternoon callers were going and coming from the houses when the mistress was "at home;" and at my door, too, soon began the usual din of bell and knocker. Joe was quite equal to the occasion, and enjoyed Friday, the day I received. Dressed in his very best, and with a collar that kept his chin in what seemed to me a fearful state of torture, but added to his height by at least half an inch, Joe stood behind the hall-door, ready to open it directly the knocker was released. He ushered in the guests as though "to the manner born," giving out the names correctly, and with all the ease of an experienced groom of the chambers.

The conservatory leading out of the drawing-room was Joe's especial pride; it was his great pleasure to syringe the hanging baskets, and attend to the ferns and plants. Many shillings from his pocket-money were spent in little surprises for me in the form of pots of musk, maiden-hair, or anything he could buy; his wages were all sent home, and he only kept for his own whatever he had given to him, and sometimes a guest would "tip" him more generously than I liked, for his bright eyes and ready hands were always at everybody's service.

After my husband's return home, who from the first became Joe's especial care, as to boots, brushing of clothes, etc., it became necessary to give two or three dinner-parties, and I must confess I felt nervous as to how Joe would acquit himself.

In our dining-room was a very large bear-skin rug, and the floor being polished oak, it was dangerous to step on this rug, for it would slip away from the feet on the smooth surface, and even the dogs avoided it, so many falls had they met with upon it.

The first day of my husband's arrival we had my sister and a friend to dine, and had been talking about Joe in the few moments before dinner.

My husband had been laughing at the size of my page, and scolding me a little, or rather pretending to do so, for taking a written character.

"Little woman," he said, "don't be surprised if one night a few country burglars make us a visit, and renew their acquaintance with Mr. J. Cole."

"You don't know Joe," I replied, "or you would never say that."

"Do you know him so well, little wife?" said my dear sensible husband; "remember he has only been in our service six months. In the country he had very little of value in his hands, but here, it seems to me, he has too much. All the plate, and indeed everything of value, is in his pantry, and he is a very young boy to trust. One of the women servants should take charge of the plate-chest, I think. Where does this paragon sleep?"

"Down-stairs," I said, "next to the kitchen, at the back of the house; and you should see how carefully every night he looks to the plate-basket, counts everything, and then asks Mrs. Wilson to see it is right, locks it up, and gives her the key to take care of. No one can either open or carry away an iron safe easily, and there is nothing else worth taking; besides, I know Joe is honest, I feel it."

"Well, I hope so, dear," was my husband's reply, but I could see he was not quite comfortable about it.

At dinner that day Joe had an accident; he was dreadfully nervous, as usual, and when waiting, he forgot to attend to my guests first, but always came to me. The parlor-maid, a new one, and not a great favorite with Joe, made matters worse by correcting him in an audible voice; and once, when somebody wanted oyster-sauce, she told Joe to hand it. The poor boy, wishing to obey quickly, forgot to give the bear-skin a wide berth, slipped on it, and in a moment had fallen full length, having in his fall deposited the contents of the sauce- tureen partly into a blue leather armchair, and the rest onto my sister's back.

The boy's consternation was dreadful. I could see he was completely overcome with fright and sorrow for what he had done. He got up, and all his trembling lips could say was, "Oh, please, I'm so sorry; it was the bear as tripped me up. I am so very sorry."

Even my husband could scarcely keep from smiling, the sorrow was so genuine, the sense of shame so true.

"There, never mind, Joe," he said kindly; "you must be more careful. Now run and get a sponge, and do the best you can with it."

After that Joe had the greatest terror of that treacherous skin, and I heard him telling the parlor-maid about it.

"You mind," he said, "or that bear'll ketch 'old of yer. I shan't forget how he ketched 'old of my leg that day and knocked me over; so you'd better take care, and not go nigher than you can 'elp. He's always a-lookin' out to ketch yer, but he won't 'ave me no more, I can tell him."

This fall of Joe's made him still more nervous of waiting at table, and at last, when he had made some very serious mistakes, I had to speak to him and tell him I was afraid, if he did not soon learn to wait better, I must send him away, for his master was annoyed at the mistakes he made, such as pouring port instead of sherry, giving cold plates when hot ones were required, handing dishes on the wrong side, etc.

My little lecture was listened to quietly and humbly, and Joe had turned to go away, when, to my surprise and distress, he suddenly burst into a perfect passion of tears and sobs.

"I will try and learn myself," he said, as well as his sobs would let him, "indeed, I will. I know I'm stoopid. I sez to myself every time company comes, 'I'll mind wot I'm about, and remember dishes left- 'anded, pour-in's out right, sherry wine's yeller, and port wine afterwards with the nuts, grapes, and things; and the cruits when there's fish, and begin with the strangerest lady next to master's side, and 'elp missus last.' I knows it all, but when they're all sittin' down, and everybody wantin' somethin', I don't know if Jane's a-goin' to giv' it 'em, or I am; and I gets stoopid, and my 'ands shakes, and somehow I can't do nothin'; but please don't send me away. I do like you and the master. I'll ask Jane to learn me better. You see if I don't. Oh, please'm, say you'll try me!"

What could I say but "yes," and for a day or two Joe did better, but we were a small party, and the waiting was easy; but shortly we were to have a large dinner-party, and as the time drew near, Joe became quite pale and anxious.

About this time, too, I had been awakened at night by curious sounds down-stairs, as of somebody moving about, and once I heard an unmistakable fall of some heavy article.

My husband assured me it was nothing alarming, and he went down- stairs, but could neither hear or see anything unusual. All was quiet.

Another night I felt sure I heard sounds down-stairs; and in spite of my husband's advice to remain still, I called Mrs. Wilson, and entreated her to come down to the kitchen-floor with me. It was so very easy, I knew, for anybody to enter the house from the back, and there being a deep area all round, they could work away with their tools at the ground-floor back windows unseen. Any one could get on the top of the stable from the mews, drop into the garden, and be safe; for the watchman and policeman were on duty in the front of the house only, the back was quite unprotected. True, there were iron bars to Joe's window and the kitchen, but iron bars could be sawed through, and I lived in dread of burglars.

This night Mrs. Wilson and I went softly down, and as we neared the kitchen stairs, I heard a voice say in a whisper, "Make haste!"

"There, Mrs. Wilson, did you hear that?" I said. "Was that imagination?"

"No, ma'am," she replied; "there's somebody talking, and I believe it's in Joe's room. Let us go up and fetch the master."

So we returned up-stairs, and soon my husband stood with us at the door of Joe's room.

"Open the door, Joe!" cried my husband. "Who have you got there?"

"Nobody, please, sir," said a trembling voice.

"Open the door at once!" said the master, and in a moment it was opened. Joe stood there very pale, but with no sort of fear in his face. There was nobody in the room, and as Joe had certainly been in bed, we concluded he must have talked in his sleep, and, perhaps, walked about also, for what we knew.

The day before the dinner-party, Cook came and told me she felt sure there was something wrong with Joe. He was so changed from what he used to be; there was no getting him to wake in the morning, and he seemed so heavy with sleep, as if he had no rest at night. Also Cook had proofs of his having been in her kitchen after he was supposed to have gone to bed; chairs were moved, and several things not where she had left them. She had asked Joe, and he replied he did go into the kitchen, but would not say what for.

I did not like to talk to Joe that day, so decided to wait till after the dinner, and I would then insist on the mystery being cleared up. I knew Joe would tell the truth;

my trust was unshaken, although circumstances seemed against him.

That night Mrs. Wilson came to my door, and said she was sure Joe was at his nightwork again, for she could see from her bedroom window a light reflected on the stable wall, which must be in his room.

"How can we find out," I said, "what he is doing?"

"That is easily done," said my husband. "We can go out at the garden- door, and down the steps leading from the garden into the area; they are opposite his window. We can look through the Venetian blinds, if they are down, and see for ourselves. He won't be able to see us."

Accordingly, having first wrapped up in our furs, we went down, and were soon at Joe's window, standing in the area that surrounded the house. The laths of the blind were some of them open, and between them we saw distinctly all over the room.

At first we could not understand the strange sight that met our gaze.

In the middle of Joe's room was a table, spread with a cloth, and on it saucers from flower-pots, placed at intervals down each side; before each saucer a chair was placed, and in the centre of the table a high basket, from which a Stilton cheese had been unpacked that morning,-this was evidently to represent a tall *epergne*. On Joe's wash-stand were several bottles, a jug, and by each flower-pot saucer two vessels of some kind--by one, two jam-pots of different sizes; by another, a broken specimen glass and a teacup--and so on; and from chair to chair moved Joe, softly but quickly, on tiptoe, now with bottles which contained water. We could see his lips move, and concluded he was saying something to imaginary persons, for he would put a jampot on his tray, and pour into it from the bottle, and then replace it. Sometimes he would go quickly to his bed, which we saw represented the dinner-wagon, or sideboard, and bring imaginary dishes from there and hand them. Then he would go quickly from chair to chair, always correcting himself if he went to the wrong side, and talking all the time softly to himself. So here was the solution of the mystery; here melted into air the visions of Joe in league with midnight burglars.

The poor boy, evidently alarmed at the prospect of the dinner-party, and feeling that he must try to improve in waiting at table before that time somehow, had stolen all those hours nightly from his rest, to practise with whatever substitutes were at hand for the usual table requisites.

Here every night, when those who had worked far less during the day were soundly sleeping, had that anxious, striving little heart shaken off fatigue, and the big blue eyes refused to yield to sleep, in order to fight with the nervousness that alone prevented his willing hands acting with their natural cleverness. I felt a choking in my throat, when I saw the thin, pale little face, that should have been on the pillow hours before, lighted up with triumph as the supposed guests departed; the dumb show of folding the dinner napkins belonging to myself and the master, and putting them in their respective rings, told us the ordeal was over. What a weird scene it was,--the dim light, the silent house, the spread table, and the empty chairs! One could imagine ghostly revellers, visible only to that one fragile attendant, who ministered so willingly to their numerous wants. The sort of nervous thrill that heralds hysterical attacks was rapidly overcoming me, and I whispered to my husband, "Let us go now;" but he lingered yet a few seconds, and silently drew my attention again to the window.

Joe was on his knees by his bedside, his face hidden in his hands. What silent prayer was ascending to the Throne of Grace, who shall say? I only know that it were well if many a kneeling worshipper in "purple and fine linen" could feel as sure of being heard as Joe did when, his victory won, he knelt, in his humble servant's garb, and said his prayers that night in spite of the aching head and weary limbs that needed so badly the few hours' rest that remained before six o'clock, the time Joe always got up.

Silently we stole away, and in my mind from that moment my faith in Joe never wavered. Not once, in spite of sad events that came to pass later on, when even I, his staunchest friend, had to recall to memory that kneeling little form in the silence of the night, alone with his God, in order to stifle the cruel doubts of his truth that were forced upon us all by circumstances I must soon relate.

The famous dinner passed off well. Joe was splendid; his midnight practice had brought its reward, and he moved about so swiftly, and anticipated everybody's wants so well, that some of my friends asked me where I got such a treasure of a page; he must have had a good butler or footman to teach him, they said; he is evidently used to waiting on many guests. I was proud of Joe.

The next day he came to me with more than a sovereign in silver, and told me the gentlemen had been so very kind to him, "and a'most every one had given him somethin', tho' he never arst, or waited about, as some fellers did, as if they wouldn't lose sight of a gent till he paid 'em. But," said Joe, "they would giv' it me; and one gent, he follered me right up the passage, he did, and sez, 'Ere, you small boy,' he sez, and he give me a whole 'arf-crown. Whatever for, I don't know."

But I knew that must have been Dr. Loring, a celebrated physician, and my husband's dearest friend. We had told him about Joe's midnight self-teaching, and he had been much interested in the story.

You little thought, Joe, the hand that patted your curly head so kindly that night would one day hold your small wrist, and count its feeble life-pulse beating slowly and yet more slowly, while we, who loved you, should watch the clever, handsome face, trying in vain to read there the blessed word "Hope."

CHAPTER IV.

And now I must confess to those--for surely there will be a few--who have felt a little interest, so far, in the fortunes of J. Cole, that a period in my story has arrived when I would fain lay down my pen, and not awaken the sleeping past, to recall the sad trouble that befell him.

I am almost an old woman now, and all this happened many years ago, when my hair was golden instead of silver. I was younger in those days, and now am peacefully and hopefully waiting God's good time for my summons. Troubles have been my lot, many and hard to bear. Loss of husband, children, dear, good friends, many by death, and some troubles harder even than those, the loss of trust, and bitter awakening to the ingratitude and worthlessness of those in whom I have trusted,--all these I have endured. Yet time and trouble have not sufficiently hardened my heart that I can write of what follows without pain. Christmas was over, and my dear husband again away for some months. As soon as I could really say, "Spring is here," we were to leave London for our country home; and Joe was constantly talking to Mrs. Wilson about his various pets, left behind in the gardener's care. There was an old jackdaw, an especial favorite of his, a miserable owl, too, who had met with an accident, resulting in the loss of an eye; a more evil-looking object than "Cyclops," as my husband christened him, I never saw. Sometimes on a dark night this one eye would gleam luridly from out the shadowy recesses of the garden, and an unearthly cry of "Hoo-oo-t," fall on the ear, enough to give one the "creeps for a hour," as Mary, the housemaid, said. But Joe loved Cyclops, or rather "Cloppy," as he called him; and the bird hopped after Joe about the garden, as if he quite returned the feeling.

All our own dogs, and two or three maimed ones, and a cat or two, more or less hideous, and indebted to Joe's mercy in rescuing them from traps, snares, etc.,--all these creatures were Joe's delight. Each week the gardener's boy wrote a few words to Joe of their health and wonderful doings, and each week Joe faithfully sent a shilling, to be laid out in food for them. Then there was Joe's especial garden, also a sort of hospital, or convalescent home rather, where many blighted, unhealthy-looking plants and shrubs, discarded by the gardener, and cast aside to be burnt on the weed-heap, had been rescued by Joe, patiently nursed and petted as it were into life again by constant care and watching, and, after being kept in pots a while, till they showed, by sending forth some tiny shoot or bud, that the sap of life was once more circulating freely, were then planted in the sheltered corner he called "his own."

What treasures awaited him in this small square of earth. What bunches of violets he would gather for the Missis; and his longing to get back to his various pets, and his garden, was the topic of conversation on many a long evening between Joe and Mrs. Wilson.

Little Bogie, the fox-terrier, was the only dog we had with us in town, and Bogie hated London. After the quiet country life, the incessant roll of carriages, tramping of horses, and callings of coachmen, shrill cab-whistles, and all the noises of a fashionable neighborhood at night during a London season, were most objectionable to Bogie; he could not rest, and often Joe got out of bed in the night, and took him in his arms, to prevent his waking all of us, with his shrill barking at the unwonted sounds.

As I have said before, I am very nervous, and the prospect of spending several more weeks in the big London house, without my husband, was far from pleasant; so I invited my widowed sister and her girls to stay with me some time longer, and made up my mind to banish my fears, and think of nothing but that the dark nights would be getting shorter and shorter, and meanwhile our house was well protected, as far as good strong bolts and chains could do so.

One night I felt more nervous than usual. I had expected a letter from America for some days past, and none had arrived. On this evening I knew the mail was due, and I waited anxiously for the last ring of the postman at ten o'clock; but I was doomed to listen in vain. There was the sharp, loud ring next door, but not at ours; and I went to my room earlier than the others, really to give way to a few tears that I could not control.

I sat by my bedroom fire, thinking, and, I am afraid, conjuring up all sorts of terrible reasons for my dear husband's silence, until I must have fallen asleep, for I awoke chilly and cramped from the uncomfortable posture I had slept in. The fire was out, and the house silent as the grave; not even a carriage passing to take up some late guest. I looked at the clock, half-past three, and then from my window. It was that "darkest hour before dawn," and I hurried into bed, and endeavored to sleep; but no, I was hopelessly wide awake. No amount of counting, or mental exercise on the subject of "sheep going through a hedge," had any effect, and I found myself lying awake, listening. Yes, I knew that I was *listening for something that I should hear before long, but I did not know what.*

"Hark! what was that?"--a sudden thud, as if something had fallen somewhere in the house; then silence, except for the loud beating of my heart, that threatened to suffocate me. "Nonsense," I said to myself, "I am foolishly nervous to-night. It is nothing here, or Bogie would bark;" so I tried again to sleep. Hush! Surely that was a footstep going up or down the stairs! I could not endure the agony of being alone any longer, but would go to my sister's room, just across the landing, and get her to come and stay the rest of the night with me. I put on my slippers and dressing-gown, and opening my door, came face to face with my sister, who was coming to me.

"Let me come in," she said, "and don't let us alarm the girls; but I feel certain something is going on down-stairs. Bogie barked furiously an hour ago, and then was suddenly silent."

"That must have been when I was asleep," I replied; "but no doubt Joe heard him, and has taken him in."

"That may be," said my sister, "but I have kept on hearing queer noises at the back of the house; they seemed in Joe's room at first. Come and listen yourself on the stairs."

It is strange, but true, that many persons, horribly nervous at the thought of danger, find all their presence of mind in full force when actually called upon to face it. So it is with me, and so it was on that night. I stood on the landing, and listened, and in a few moments heard muffled sounds down-stairs, like persons moving about stealthily.

"There is certainly somebody down there, Nelly," I said to my sister, "and they are down in the basement. If we could creep down quietly and get into the drawing-room, we might open the window and call the watchman or policeman; both are on duty until seven."

"But think," said my sister, "of the fright of the girls if they hear us, and find they are left alone. The servants, too, will scream, and rush about, as they always do. Let us go down and make sure there are thieves, and then see what is best to be done. The door at the top of the kitchen stairs is locked, so they must be down there; and perhaps if we could get the watchman to come in quietly, we might catch them in a trap, by letting him through the drawing-room, and into the conservatory. He could get into the garden from there, and as they must have got in that way from the mews, over the stable wall, and through the garden, they would try to escape the same way, and the watchman would be waiting for them, and cut off their retreat."

I agreed, and we stole down-stairs into the drawing-room, where we locked ourselves in, then very gently and carefully drew up one of the side blinds of the bay window. The morning had begun to break, and everything in the wide road was distinctly visible. In the distance I could see the policeman on duty, but on the opposite side, and going away from our house instead of towards it. He would turn the corner at the top of the road, and go past the houses parallel with the backs of our row, and then appear at the opposite end of the park, and come along our side; there was no intermediate turning-- nothing but an unbroken row of about forty detached houses facing each other.

What could we do? I dared not wait until the policeman came back; quite twenty minutes must pass before then, and day being so near at hand, the light was increasing every moment, and the burglars would surely not leave without visiting the drawing-room and dining-room, and would perhaps murder us to save themselves from detection.

If I could only attract the policeman's attention, but how?

My sister was close to the door listening, and every instant we dreaded hearing them coming up the kitchen stairs. I could not understand Bogie not barking, and Joe not waking, for where I was I could distinctly hear the men moving about in the pantry and kitchen.

"I wonder," I said to my sister, "if I could put something across from this balcony to the stonework by the front steps? It seems such a little distance, and if I could step across, I could open the front gate in an instant, and run after the police-man. I shall try."

"You will fall and kill yourself," my sister said; "the space is much wider than you think."

But I was determined to try; for if I let that policeman go out of sight, what horrors might happen in the twenty minutes before he would come back.

The idea of one of the girls waking and calling out, or Joe waking and being shot or stabbed, gave me a feeling of desperation, as though I alone could and must save them.

Luckily the house was splendidly built, every window-sash sliding noiselessly and easily in its groove. I opened the one nearest to the hall door steps, and saw that the stone ledge abutted to within about two feet of the low balcony of the window; but I was too nervous to trust myself to spring across even that distance. At that moment my sister whispered:--

"I hear somebody coming up the kitchen stairs!"

Desperately I cast my eyes round the room for something to bridge the open space, that would bear my weight, if only for a moment. The fender-stool caught my eye; that might do, it was strong, and more than long enough. In an instant we had it across, and I was out of the window and down the front steps.

As I turned the handle of the heavy iron gate, I looked down at the front kitchen window. A man stood in the kitchen, and he looked up and saw me--such a horrible-looking ruffian, too. Fear lent wings to my feet, and I flew up the road. The watchman was just entering the park from the opposite end; he saw me, and sounded his whistle; the policeman turned and ran towards me. I was too exhausted to speak, and he caught me, just as, having gasped "Thieves at 50!" (the number of our house), I fell forward in a dead swoon.

When I recovered, I was lying on my own bed, my sister, the scared servants, and the policeman, all around me. From them I heard that directly the man in the kitchen caught sight of me, he warned his companion, who was busy forcing the lock of the door at the head of the kitchen stairs, and my sister heard them both rushing across the garden, where they had a ladder against the stable-wall. They must have pulled this up after them, and tossed it into the next garden, where it was found, to delay pursuit. The park-keeper had, after sounding his whistle, rushed to our house, got in at the window, and ran to the door at the top of the kitchen stairs, but it was quite impossible to open it; the burglars had cleverly left something in the lock when disturbed, and the key would not turn. He then went through the drawing-room into the conservatory, where a glass door opened on the garden; but by the time the heavy sliding glass panel was unfastened, and the inner door un-bolted, the men had disappeared. They took with them much less than they hoped to have done, for there were parcels and packets of spoons, forks, and a case of very handsome gold salt-cellars, a marriage gift, always kept in a baize- lined chest in the pantry, the key of which I retained, and which chest was supposed until now to be proof against burglars; the lock had been burnt all round with some instru-ment, most likely a poker heated in the gas, and then forced inwards from the burnt woodwork.

"How was it," I asked, "Joe did not wake during all this, or Bogie bark?"

As I asked the question, I noticed that my sister turned away; and Mrs. Wilson, after vainly endeavoring to look unconcerned, threw her apron suddenly over her head, and burst out crying.

"What is the matter?" I said, sitting up; "what are you all hiding from me? Send Joe to me; I will learn the truth from him."

At this the policeman came forward, and then I heard that Joe was missing, his room was in great disorder, and one of his shoes, evidently dropped in his hurry, had been found in the garden, near some spoons thrown down by the thieves; his clothes were gone, so he evidently had dressed himself after pretending to go to bed as usual; his blankets and sheets were taken away, used no doubt, the policeman said, to wrap up the stolen things.

"Is it possible," I asked, "that you suspect Joe is in league with these burglars?"

"Well, mum," said the man, "it looks queer, and very like it. He slept down-stairs close to the very door where they got in; he never gives no alarm, he must have been expecting something, or else why was he dressed? And how did his shoe come in the garden? And what's more to the point, if so be as he's innercent, where is he? These young rascals is that artful, you'd be surprised to know the dodges they're up to."

"But," I interrupted, "it is impossible, it is cruel to suspect him. He is gone, true enough, but I'm sure he will come back. Perhaps he ran after the men to try and catch them, and dropped his shoe then."

"That's not likely, mum," said he, with a pitying smile at my ignorance of cir-cumstantial evidence; "he'd have called out to stop 'em, and it 'aint likely they'd have let him get up their ladder, afore chucking of it into the next garden, if so be as he was a- chasing of 'em to get 'em took. No, mar'm; I'm very sorry, particular as you seem so kindly disposed; but, in my humble opinion, he's a artful young dodger, and this 'ere job has been planned ever so long, and he's connived at it, and has hooked it along with his pals. I knows 'em, but we'll soon nab him; and if so be as you'll be so kind as to let me take down in writin' all you knows about 'J. Cole,' which is his name, I'm informed, where you took him from, his character, and pre-vious career, it will help considerable in laying hands on him; and when he's found we'll soon find his pals."

Of course, I told all I knew about Joe. I felt positive he would come back, per-haps in a few minutes, to explain everything. Besides, there was Bogie, too. Why should he take Bogie? The policeman suggested that "perhaps the dawg foller'd him, and he had taken it along with him, to prevent being traced by its means."

At length, all this questioning being over, the household settled down into a sort of strange calm. It seemed to us days since we had said "Good-night," and sought our rooms on that night, and yet it was only twenty-four hours ago; in that short time how much had taken place! On going over all the plate, etc., we missed many more things; and Mrs. Wilson, whose faith in Joe's honesty never wavered, began to think the poor boy might have been frightened at having slept through the robbery; and as he was so proud of having the plate used every day in his charge, when he discovered it had been stolen, he might have feared we should blame him so much for it, that he had run away home to his people in his fright, meaning to ask his father, or his adored Dick, to return to me and plead for him. I thought, too, this was possible, for I knew how terribly he would reproach himself for letting anything in his care be stolen. I therefore made up my mind to telegraph to his father at once; but, not to alarm him, I said:--

"Is Joe with you? Have reason to think he has gone home. Answer back."

The answer came some hours after, for in those small villages communication was difficult. The reply ran thus:--

"We have not seen Joe; if he comes to-night will write at once. Hoping there is nothing wrong."

So that surmise was a mistake, for Joe had money, and would go by train if he went home, and be there in two hours.

All the household sat up nearly all that night, or rested uncomfortably on sofas and armchairs; we felt too unsettled to go to bed, though worn out with suspense, and the previous excitement and fright. Officials and detectives came and went during the evening, and looked about for traces of the robbers, and before night a description of the stolen things, and a most minute one of Joe, were posted outside the police-stations, and all round London for miles. A reward of twenty pounds was offered for Joe, and my heart ached to know there was a hue and cry after him like a common thief.

What would the old parents think? and how would Dick feel?--Dick whose good counsels and careful training had made Joe what I *knew* he was, in spite of every suspicion.

The next day I still felt sure he would come, and I went down into the room where he used to sleep, and saw Mrs. Wilson had put all in order, and fresh blankets sheets were on the little bed, all ready for him. So many things put me in mind of the loving, gentle disposition. A little flower-vase I valued very much had been broken by Bogie romping with one of my nieces, and knocking it down. It was broken in more than twenty pieces; and after I had patiently tried to mend it myself, and my nieces, with still greater patience, had had their turn at it, we had given it up as a bad job, and thought it had long ago gone onto the dust-heap.

There were some shelves on the wall of Joe's room where his treasures were kept; and on one of these shelves, covered with an old white handkerchief, was a little tray containing the vase, a bottle of cement, and a camel's-hair brush. The mending was finished, all but two or three of the smallest pieces, and beautifully done; it must have taken time, and an amount of patience that put my efforts and those of the girls to shame; but Joe's was a labor of love, and did not weary him. He would probably have put it in its usual place one morning, when mended, and said nothing about it until I found it out, and then confessed, in his own queer way, "Please, I knew you was sorry it was broke, and so I mended it;" then he would have hurried away, flushed with pleasure at my few words of thanks and praise.

On the mantelpiece were more of Joe's treasures, four or five cheap photographs, the subjects quite characteristic of Joe. One of them was a religious subject, "The Shepherd with a little lamb on his shoulders." A silent prayer went up from my heart that somewhere that same Good Shepherd was finding lost Joe, and bringing him safely back to us.

There were some pebbles he had picked up during a memorable trip to Margate with Dick, a year before I saw him; which pebbles he firmly believed were real "aggits," and had promised to have them polished soon, and made into brooch and earrings for Mrs. Wilson.

There was a very old-fashioned photograph of myself that I had torn in half, and thrown into the waste-paper basket. I saw this had been carefully joined together and enclosed in a cheap frame--the only one that could boast of being so preserved. I suppose Joe could only afford one frame, and his sense of the fitness of things made him choose the Missis's picture to be first honored.

How sad I felt looking round the room! People may smile at my feeling so sad and concerned about a servant, a common, lowborn page-boy. Ay, smile on, if you will, but tell me, my friend, can you say, if you were in Joe's position at that time, with circumstantial evidence so strong against you, poor and lowly as he was, are there four or five, or even two or three of your friends who would believe in you, stand up for you, and trust in you, in spite of all, as we did for Joe?

I had gone up to my sitting-room, after telling Mary to light the fire in poor Joe's room, and let it look warm and cosey; for I had some sort of presentiment that I should see the poor boy again very soon--how, I knew not, but I have all my life been subject to spiritual influences, and have seldom been mistaken in them.

We were all thinking of going early to rest, for since the robbery none of us had had any real sleep. Suddenly the front door-bell rang timidly, as if the visitor were not quite sure of its being right to pull the handle.

"Perhaps that's Joe," said my sister.

But I knew Joe would not ring that bell.

We heard Mary open the door, and a man's voice ask if Mr. Aylmer lived there.

"Yes," said Mary, "but he is abroad; but you can see Mrs. Aylmer." Then came a low murmuring of voices, and Mary came in, saying:--

"Oh, ma'am, it's Dick, Joe's brother; and he says may he see you?"

"Send him in here at once," I replied.

And in a moment Dick stood before me--Dick, Joe's beau-ideal of all that was good, noble, and to be admired. I must say the mind-picture I had formed of Dick was totally unlike the reality. I had expected to see a sunburnt, big fellow, with broad shoulders and expressive features.

The real Dick was a thin, delicate-looking young man, with a pale face, and black straight hair. He stood with his hat in his hand, looking down as if afraid to speak.

"Oh, pray come in," I cried, going forward to meet him. "I know who you are. Oh, have you brought me any news of poor Joe? We are all his friends here, his true friends, and you must let us be yours too in this trouble. Have you seen him?"

At my words the bowed head was lifted up, and then I saw Dick's face as it was. If ever truth, honor, and generosity looked out from the windows of a soul, they looked out of those large blue eyes of Dick's--eyes so exactly like Joe's in expression, that the black lashes instead of the fair ones seemed wrong somehow.

"God bless you, lady, for them words," said Dick; and before I could prevent it, he had knelt at my feet, caught my hand and pressed it to his lips, while wild sobs broke from him.

"Forgive me," he said, rising to his feet, and leaning with one hand on the back of a chair, his whole frame shaking with emotion. "Forgive me for givin' way like this; but I've seen them papers about our Joe, and I know what's being thought of him, and I've come here ashamed to see you, thinkin' you believed as the rest do, that Joe robbed you after all your goodness to him. Why, lady, I tell you, rather than I'd believe that of my little lad, as I thrashed till my heart almost broke to hear him sob, for the only lie as he ever told in all his life; if I could believe it, I'd take father's old gun and end my life, for I'd be a beast, not fit to live any longer. And I thought you doubted him too; but now I hear you say you're his friend, and believes in him, and don't think he robbed you, I know now there's good folks in the world, and there's mercy and justice, and it ain't all wrong, as I'd come a'most to think as it was, when I first know'd about this 'ere."

"Sit down, Dick," I said, "and recover yourself, and let us see what can be done. I will tell you all that has happened, and then perhaps you can throw some light on Joe's conduct--you who know him so well."

Dick sat down, and shading his eyes with his hand that his tears might not betray his weakness any more, he listened quietly while I went over all the events of that dreadful night.

When I had finished, Dick sat for some moments quite silent, then with a weary gesture, passing his hand across his forehead, he remarked sadly:--

"I can't make nothing of it; it's a thing beyond my understanding. I'm that dazed like, I can't see nothin' straight. However, what I've got to do is to find Joe, and that I mean to do; if he's alive I'll find him, and then let him speak for hisself. I don't believe he's done nothing wrong, but if he has done ever so little or ever so much, he'll 'own up to it whatever it is,' that's what Joe'll do. I told him to lay by them words and hold to 'em, and I'll lay my life he'll do as I told him. I've got a bed down Marylebone way, at my aunt's what's married to a policeman; I'm to stay there, and I'll have a talk with 'em about this and get some advice. I know Joe's innercent, and why don't he come and say so? But I'll find him."

I inquired about the old people, and how they bore their trial.

"Father's a'most beside hisself," said Dick; "and only that he's got to keep mother in the dark about this, he'd have come with me; but mother, she's a-bed with rheumatics, and doctor told father her heart was weak-like, and she mustn't be told, or it would p'raps kill her. She thinks a deal of Joe, does mother, being the youngest, and always such a sort of lovin' little chap he were." And here Dick's voice broke again, and I made him go down to Mrs. Wilson, and have some refreshment before leaving, and he promised to see me again the first thing in the morning, when he had talked to his friend, the policeman.

Scarcely had Dick gone, when a loud, and this time firm ring, announced another visitor, and in a cab, too, I could hear. Evidently there was no going to rest early that night, as ten o'clock was then striking.

Soon, to my surprise, I heard a well-known voice, and Mary announced Dr. Loring, my husband's old friend, of whom I have already spoken.

"Well, my dear," he cried, in his pleasant, cheerful voice, that in itself seemed to lift some of the heaviness from my heart, "are you not astonished to see me at such an hour?"

"Astonished, certainly," I replied; "but very, very glad. You are always welcome; and more than ever now, when we are in trouble and sorrow. Do sit down, and stay with me awhile."

"Yes, I will, for an hour, gladly," he said. "But there's something outside that had better be brought in first. You know I've only just arrived from Devonshire, and there are two barrels of Devonshire apples on that cab, one for you, and one for the wife, that is why you see me here; for I thought it would not be ten minutes out of my road to pass by here, and leave them with you, and so save the trouble of sending them by carrier to-morrow."

I rang for Mary, and the doctor suggested the apples being put somewhere where the smell of them could not penetrate up-stairs; for, as he truly remarked, "Though a fine ripe pippin is delicious to eat at breakfast or luncheon, the smell of them shut up in a house is horrible."

"I dare say Mrs. Wilson will find a place in the basement," I said; "for we don't use half the room there is down there."

Having ordered the barrel to be stowed away, I soon settled my visitor comfortably in an armchair by the fire, with a cup of his favorite cocoa by his side.

"And now, my dear," said he, "tell me about this burglary that has taken place, and which has made you look as if you wanted me to take care of you a while, and bring back some color to your pale cheeks. And what about this boy? Is it the same queer little fellow who chose midnight to play his pranks in once before? I'm not often deceived in a face, and I thought his was an honest one. I"--

"So it was," I interrupted; "don't say a word until I've told you all, and you will"--

I had scarcely begun speaking, when a succession of the most fearful screams arose from down-stairs, each rising louder and louder, in the extreme of terror. My sister, who had gone to her room, rushed down to me; the girls, in their dressing-gowns, just as they were preparing for bed, followed, calling out, "Auntie! O Auntie! what is it? Who is screaming? What can be the matter?" Hardly were they in the room when Mary rushed in, ghastly, her eyes staring, and in a voice hoarse with terror, gasped out, "Come! come! he's found! he's murdered! I saw him. He's lying in the cellar, with his throat cut. Oh, it's horrible!" Then she began to scream again.

The doctor tried to hold me back, but I broke from him, and ran down-stairs, where I could find no one; all was dark in the kitchens, but there was a light in the area, and I was soon there, followed by Dr. Loring.

By the open cellar-door stood Mrs. Wilson, and the cabman with her. Directly she saw me, she called out, "Oh, dear mistress, don't you come here; it's not a sight for you. Take her away, Dr. Loring, she musn't see it."

"What is it?" I cried; "Mary says it's"--I could not say the words, but seizing the candle from Mrs. Wilson's hand, I went into the cellar.

The good doctor was close to me, with more light, by the aid of which we beheld, in the far corner, facing us, what seemed to be a bundle of blankets, from which protruded a head, a horrible red stream surrounding it, and flowing, as it were, from the open mouth. One second brought me close. It was Joe--Joe, with his poor limbs bound with cruel ropes, and in his mouth for a gag they had forced one of those bright red socks he would always wear. Thank God, it was only that red sock, and not the horrible red stream I had feared. He was dead, of course; but not such a fearful death as that.

The doctor soon pulled the horrid gag from his mouth, and the good- natured cabman, who evidently felt for us, helped to cut the ropes, and lift up the poor cold little form.

As they lifted him, something that was in the blankets fell heavily to the ground. It was poor Bogie's dead body, stabbed in many places, each wound enough to have let out the poor dumb creature's life.

By this time help had arrived, and once more the police took possession of us, as it were.

Of course, *now* everything was explained. The burglars had evidently entered Joe's room, and Bogie, being in his arms, had barked, and wakened him. A few blows had soon silenced poor Bogie, and a gag and cords had done the same for Joe.

When the man saw me from the kitchen window he must have known that help would soon come, and to prevent Joe giving information too soon they had hastily seized him, bed-clothes and all, and put him into that cellar, to starve if he were not discovered.

Perhaps they did not really mean to kill the poor child, and if we had been in the habit of using that cellar we might have found him in a few hours or less; but, unfortunately, it was a place we never used, it reached far under the street, and was too large for our use. Our coal-cellar was a much smaller one, inside the scullery; the door of poor Joe's prison closed with a common latch.

Had there been any doubt in the detective's mind as to Joe's guilt, he might have taken more trouble, and searched for him, even there; but from the first everybody but ourselves had been sure Joe had escaped with the burglars, so the cellar remained unsearched.

Mrs. Wilson, wishing to spare me the smell of the apples, thought that cellar, being outside the house, a very suitable place for them, and on opening the door had caught sight of something in the distant corner, and sent Mary to see what it was. Then arose those fearful shrieks we had heard, and Mary had rushed out of the cellar half mad with fright.

In less time than it has taken me to relate this, Joe was laid on the rug before the drawing-room fire, and I summoned courage to look on the changed face.

"Could that be Joe--so white, so drawn, so still?"

Dr. Loring was kneeling by the little form, chafing and straightening the poor stiffened arms, so bent with their cruel pinioning behind the shoulders.

"Doctor," I said, "why do you do any more? Nothing can bring back the poor fellow, murdered while doing his duty." Then I, too, knelt down, and took the poor cold hands in mine,

"Oh, my poor child!" I cried, "my little brave heart; who dared say you were false? Let those who doubted you look at you now, with dry eyes, if they can."

"My dear," said Dr. Loring suddenly, "have you always hot water in your bath-room?"

"Yes, doctor," I said; "yes. Why do you ask? Do you mean--is it possible--there is life?" And I took Joe's little head in my arms, and forgot he was only a servant, only a poor, common little page- boy. I only know I pressed him to my breast, and called him by all the endearing names I used to call my own children in after years, when God gave me some, and kissed his white forehead in my joy at the blessed ray of hope.

No want of willing arms to carry Joe up-stairs. Mrs. Wilson had the bath filled before the doctor was in the room with his light burden.

"A few drops of brandy, to moisten the lips, first of all," said the good doctor, "then the bath and gentle friction; there is certainly life in him."

Now my good sister's clever nursing proved invaluable. All that night we fought every inch of ground, as it were, with our grim enemy; the dear, good doctor never relaxed in his efforts to bring back life to the cramped limbs. The burglars had un-knowingly helped to keep alight Joe's feeble spark of life by wrapping the blankets round him; they had meant, no doubt, to stifle any sound he might make; but by keeping him from actual contact with the stone floor, and protecting him from the cold, they had given him his little chance of life.

Oh, how I blessed that kind thought of Dr. Loring's to bring me a barrel of apples! Had there been no occasion to open the cellar-door, Joe would have died before another morning had dawned, died! starved! What a horrible death! And to know that within a few steps were food, warmth, and kind hearts--hearts even then saddened by his absence, and grieving for him. What hours of agony he must have passed in the cold and darkness, hearing the footsteps of passers-by above his living tomb, and feeling the pangs of hunger and thirst. What weeks those three days must have seemed to him in their fearful darkness, until insensibility mercifully came to his aid, and hushed his senses to oblivion.

Morning was far advanced when, at last, Joe's eyelids began to flutter, and his eyes opened a very little, to close again immediately; even the subdued light we had let into the room being too much for him to bear after so long a darkness; but in that brief glance he had recognized me, and seeing his lips move, I bent my head close to them.

Only a faint murmuring came, but I distinguished the words:

"Missis, I couldn't 'elp it! Forgive me. Say 'Our Father.'"

I knelt down, and as well as I could for the tears that almost choked me, re-peated that most simple, yet all-satisfying petition to the Throne of Grace.

Meanwhile the doctor held Joe's wrist, and my sister, at a sign from him, put a few drops of nourishment between the pale lips.

"My dear," at length said the doctor, "did you say the boy's brother was in London?"

"Yes," I replied, "but I have no address, as I expect him here this morning."

"That is well; he may be in time."

"In time?" I repeated; "in time for what? Is he dying? Can nothing be done?"

The good doctor looked again with moistened eyes on the little white face, and said sadly--

"I fear not, but the sight of this brother he seems to have such a strong love for may rouse him for a while. As it is, he is sinking fast. I can do no more, he is beyond human skill; but love and God's help may yet save him. Poor little fellow, he has done his duty nobly, and even to die doing *that* is an enviable fate; but we want such boys as this to live, and show others the way."

There was a slight sound at the room door, and on turning round I saw Dick--Dick with wild, dumb entreaty in his eyes.

I pointed to the bed, and with a whispered "Hush!" beckoned him to enter.

The shock of seeing his loved little lad so changed was too much for even his man's courage, for, with a cry he in vain strove to smother, he sunk on his knees with his face hidden in his hands.

But only for a moment he let his grief overcome him; then, rising, he took Joe's little form in his arms, and in a voice to which love gave the softest and gentlest tones said:--

"Joe, lad! Joe, little chap! here's Dick. Look at poor old Dick. Don't you know him? Don't go away without sayin' good-by to Dick wot loves you."

Slowly a little fluttering smile parted the lips, and the blue eyes unclosed once more. "Dick!" he gasped; "I wanted to tell you, Dick, but--I--can't. I--ain't--forgot. 'Own--up--to--it--wotever'--I minded it all. Kiss me--Dick. God--bless--missis. Dick--take me--home--to-- mother!"

And with a gentle sigh, in the arms of the brother he loved, Joe fell into a deep sleep, a sleep from which we all feared he would no more awake on earth, and we watched him, fearing almost to move.

Dick held him in his arms all that morning, and presently towards noon the doctor took the little wrist, and found the pulse still feebly beating; a smile lit up his good, kind face, and he whispered to me, "There is hope."

"Thank God!" I whispered back, and ran away into my own room to sob out grateful prayers of thanksgiving to Heaven for having spared the life so nearly lost to us.

When I went back, Joe had just begun to awaken, and was looking up into his beloved Dick's face, murmuring: "Why, it's Dick. Are you a- crying about *me*, Dick? Don't cry--I'm all right--I'm only so tired."

And having drank some wine the doctor had ordered should be given him, he nestled close to Dick's breast, and again fell into a sweet sleep, a better, life-giving sleep this time, for the faint color came to his pale little lips, and presently Dick laid him down on the pillows, and rested his own weary arms. He would not move from Joe's side for fear, he might wake and miss him, but for many hours our little fellow slept peacefully, and so gradually came back to life.

We never quite knew the particulars of the robbery, for, when Joe was well enough to talk, we avoided speaking of it. Dr. Loring said, "The boy only partly remembers it, like a dream, and it is better he should forget it altogether; he will do so when he gets stronger. Send him home to his mother for a while; and if he returns to you, let it be to the country house where there is nothing to remind him of all this."

Joe did get strong, and came back to us, but no longer as a page-boy; he was under-gardener, and his time was spent among his favorite flowers and pet animals, until one day Dick wrote to say his father had bought more land to be laid out in gardens, and if Joe could be spared he and Dick could work together, and in time set up for themselves in the business.

So Joe left us, but not to forget us, or be forgotten. On each anniversary of my birthday I find a bunch of magnificent roses on my breakfast table--"With J. and R. Cole's respectful duty," and I know the sender is a fine, strong young market-gardener; but sometimes I look back a few years, and instead of the lovely roses, and the big, healthy giver, I seem to see a faded dusty bunch of wild-flowers, held towards me by the little hot hand of a tired child with large blue eyes, and I hear a timid voice say, "Please'm, it's J. Cole; and I've come to stay with yer!"

The Codes Of Hammurabi And Moses
W. W. Davies

QTY

The discovery of the Hammurabi Code is one of the greatest achievements of archaeology, and is of paramount interest, not only to the student of the Bible, but also to all those interested in ancient history...

Religion   **ISBN:** *1-59462-338-4*   **Pages:132**
MSRP $12.95

The Theory of Moral Sentiments
Adam Smith

QTY

This work from 1749. contains original theories of conscience amd moral judgment and it is the foundation for systemof morals.

Philosophy   ISBN: *1-59462-777-0*   **Pages:536**
MSRP $19.95

Jessica's First Prayer
Hesba Stretton

QTY

In a screened and secluded corner of one of the many railway-bridges which span the streets of London there could be seen a few years ago, from five o'clock every morning until half past eight, a tidily set-out coffee-stall, consisting of a trestle and board, upon which stood two large tin cans, with a small fire of charcoal burning under each so as to keep the coffee boiling during the early hours of the morning when the work-people were thronging into the city on their way to their daily toil...

Pages:84

Childrens   ISBN: *1-59462-373-2*   *MSRP $9.95*

My Life and Work
Henry Ford

QTY

Henry Ford revolutionized the world with his implementation of mass production for the Model T automobile. Gain valuable business insight into his life and work with his own auto-biography... "We have only started on our development of our country we have not as yet, with all our talk of wonderful progress, done more than scratch the surface. The progress has been wonderful enough but..."

Pages:300

Biographies/   ISBN: *1-59462-198-5*   *MSRP $21.95*

The Art of Cross-Examination
Francis Wellman

QTY

I presume it is the experience of every author, after his first book is published upon an important subject, to be almost overwhelmed with a wealth of ideas and illustrations which could readily have been included in his book, and which to his own mind, at least, seem to make a second edition inevitable. Such certainly was the case with me; and when the first edition had reached its sixth impression in five months, I rejoiced to learn that it seemed to my publishers that the book had met with a sufficiently favorable reception to justify a second and considerably enlarged edition. ..

Pages:412

Reference   ISBN: *1-59462-647-2*   *MSRP $19.95*

On the Duty of Civil Disobedience
Henry David Thoreau

QTY

Thoreau wrote his famous essay, On the Duty of Civil Disobedience, as a protest against an unjust but popular war and the immoral but popular institution of slave-owning. He did more than write—he declined to pay his taxes, and was hauled off to gaol in consequence. Who can say how much this refusal of his hastened the end of the war and of slavery ?

Law   ISBN: *1-59462-747-9*   **Pages:48**

MSRP $7.45

Dream Psychology Psychoanalysis for Beginners
Sigmund Freud

QTY

Sigmund Freud, born Sigismund Schlomo Freud (May 6, 1856 - September 23, 1939), was a Jewish-Austrian neurologist and psychiatrist who co-founded the psychoanalytic school of psychology. Freud is best known for his theories of the unconscious mind, especially involving the mechanism of repression; his redefinition of sexual desire as mobile and directed towards a wide variety of objects; and his therapeutic techniques, especially his understanding of transference in the therapeutic relationship and the presumed value of dreams as sources of insight into unconscious desires.

Pages:196

Psychology   ISBN: *1-59462-905-6*   *MSRP $15.45*

The Miracle of Right Thought
Orison Swett Marden

QTY

Believe with all of your heart that you will do what you were made to do. When the mind has once formed the habit of holding cheerful, happy, prosperous pictures, it will not be easy to form the opposite habit. It does not matter how improbable or how far away this realization may see, or how dark the prospects may be, if we visualize them as best we can, as vividly as possible, hold tenaciously to them and vigorously struggle to attain them, they will gradually become actualized, realized in the life. But a desire, a longing without endeavor, a yearning abandoned or held indifferently will vanish without realization.

Pages:360

Self Help   ISBN: *1-59462-644-8*   *MSRP $25.45*

QTY

The Rosicrucian Cosmo-Conception Mystic Christianity *by Max Heindel*　ISBN: *1-59462-188-8*　**$38.95**
The Rosicrucian Cosmo-conception is not dogmatic, neither does it appeal to any other authority than the reason of the student. It is: not controversial, but is: sent forth in the, hope that it may help to clear...　New Age/Religion Pages 646

Abandonment To Divine Providence *by Jean-Pierre de Caussade*　ISBN: *1-59462-228-0*　**$25.95**
"The Rev. Jean Pierre de Caussade was one of the most remarkable spiritual writers of the Society of Jesus in France in the 18th Century. His death took place at Toulouse in 1751. His works have gone through many editions and have been republished...　Inspirational/Religion Pages 400

Mental Chemistry *by Charles Haanel*　ISBN: *1-59462-192-6*　**$23.95**
Mental Chemistry allows the change of material conditions by combining and appropriately utilizing the power of the mind. Much like applied chemistry creates something new and unique out of careful combinations of chemicals the mastery of mental chemistry...　New Age Pages 354

The Letters of Robert Browning and Elizabeth Barret Barrett 1845-1846 vol II　ISBN: *1-59462-193-4*　**$35.95**
by Robert Browning and Elizabeth Barrett　Biographies Pages 596

Gleanings In Genesis (volume I) *by Arthur W. Pink*　ISBN: *1-59462-130-6*　**$27.45**
Appropriately has Genesis been termed "the seed plot of the Bible" for in it we have, in germ form, almost all of the great doctrines which are afterwards fully developed in the books of Scripture which follow...　Religion/Inspirational Pages 420

The Master Key *by L. W. de Laurence*　ISBN: *1-59462-001-6*　**$30.95**
In no branch of human knowledge has there been a more lively increase of the spirit of research during the past few years than in the study of Psychology, Concentration and Mental Discipline. The requests for authentic lessons in Thought Control, Mental Discipline and...　New Age/Business Pages 422

The Lesser Key Of Solomon Goetia *by L. W. de Laurence*　ISBN: *1-59462-092-X*　**$9.95**
This translation of the first book of the "Lemegton" which is now for the first time made accessible to students of Talismanic Magic was done, after careful collation and edition, from numerous Ancient Manuscripts in Hebrew, Latin, and French...　New Age/Occult Pages 92

Rubaiyat Of Omar Khayyam *by Edward Fitzgerald*　ISBN:*1-59462-332-5*　**$13.95**
Edward Fitzgerald, whom the world has already learned, in spite of his own efforts to remain within the shadow of anonymity, to look upon as one of the rarest poets of the century, was born at Bredfield, in Suffolk, on the 31st of March, 1809. He was the third son of John Purcell...　Music Pages 172

Ancient Law *by Henry Maine*　ISBN: *1-59462-128-4*　**$29.95**
The chief object of the following pages is to indicate some of the earliest ideas of mankind, as they are reflected in Ancient Law, and to point out the relation of those ideas to modern thought.　Religiom/History Pages 452

Far-Away Stories *by William J. Locke*　ISBN: *1-59462-129-2*　**$19.45**
"Good wine needs no bush, but a collection of mixed vintages does. And this book is just such a collection. Some of the stories I do not want to remain buried for ever in the museum files of dead magazine-numbers an author's not unpardonable vanity..."　Fiction Pages 272

Life of David Crockett *by David Crockett*　ISBN: *1-59462-250-7*　**$27.45**
"Colonel David Crockett was one of the most remarkable men of the times in which he lived. Born in humble life, but gifted with a strong will, an indomitable courage, and unremitting perseverance...　Biographies/New Age Pages 424

Lip-Reading *by Edward Nitchie*　ISBN: *1-59462-206-X*　**$25.95**
Edward B. Nitchie, founder of the New York School for the Hard of Hearing, now the Nitchie School of Lip-Reading, Inc, wrote "LIP-READING Principles and Practice". The development and perfecting of this meritorious work on lip-reading was an undertaking...　How-to Pages 400

A Handbook of Suggestive Therapeutics, Applied Hypnotism, Psychic Science　ISBN: *1-59462-214-0*　**$24.95**
by Henry Munro　Health/New Age/Health/Self-help Pages 376

A Doll's House: and Two Other Plays *by Henrik Ibsen*　ISBN: *1-59462-112-8*　**$19.95**
Henrik Ibsen created this classic when in revolutionary 1848 Rome. Introducing some striking concepts in playwriting for the realist genre, this play has been studied the world over.　Fiction/Classics/Plays 308

The Light of Asia *by sir Edwin Arnold*　ISBN: *1-59462-204-3*　**$13.95**
In this poetic masterpiece, Edwin Arnold describes the life and teachings of Buddha. The man who was to become known as Buddha to the world was born as Prince Gautama of India but he rejected the worldly riches and abandoned the reigns of power when...　Religion/History/Biographies Pages 170

The Complete Works of Guy de Maupassant *by Guy de Maupassant*　ISBN: *1-59462-157-8*　**$16.95**
"For days and days, nights and nights, I had dreamed of that first kiss which was to consecrate our engagement, and I knew not on what spot I should put my lips...　Fiction/Classics Pages 240

The Art of Cross-Examination *by Francis L. Wellman*　ISBN: *1-59462-309-0*　**$26.95**
Written by a renowned trial lawyer, Wellman imparts his experience and uses case studies to explain how to use psychology to extract desired information through questioning.　How-to/Science/Reference Pages 408

Answered or Unanswered? *by Louisa Vaughan*　ISBN: *1-59462-248-5*　**$10.95**
Miracles of Faith in China　Religion Pages 112

The Edinburgh Lectures on Mental Science (1909) *by Thomas*　ISBN: *1-59462-008-3*　**$11.95**
This book contains the substance of a course of lectures recently given by the writer in the Queen Street Hail, Edinburgh. Its purpose is to indicate the Natural Principles governing the relation between Mental Action and Material Conditions...　New Age/Psychology Pages 148

Ayesha *by H. Rider Haggard*　ISBN: *1-59462-301-5*　**$24.95**
Verily and indeed it is the unexpected that happens! Probably if there was one person upon the earth from whom the Editor of this, and of a certain previous history, did not expect to hear again...　Classics Pages 380

Ayala's Angel *by Anthony Trollope*　ISBN: *1-59462-352-X*　**$29.95**
The two girls were both pretty, but Lucy who was twenty-one who supposed to be simple and comparatively unattractive, whereas Ayala was credited, as her Bombwhat romantic name might show, with poetic charm and a taste for romance. Ayala when her father died was nineteen...　Fiction Pages 484

The American Commonwealth *by James Bryce*　ISBN: *1-59462-286-8*　**$34.45**
An interpretation of American democratic political theory. It examines political mechanics and society from the perspective of Scotsman James Bryce　Politics Pages 572

Stories of the Pilgrims *by Margaret P. Pumphrey*　ISBN: *1-59462-116-0*　**$17.95**
This book explores pilgrims religious oppression in England as well as their escape to Holland and eventual crossing to America on the Mayflower, and their early days in New England...　History Pages 268

QTY

The Fasting Cure *by Sinclair Upton*   ISBN: *1-59462-222-1*   **$13.95**
In the Cosmopolitan Magazine for May, 1910, and in the Contemporary Review (London) for April, 1910, I published an article dealing with my experiences in fasting. I have written a great many magazine articles, but never one which attracted so much attention... New Age/Self Help/Health Pages 164

Hebrew Astrology *by Sepharial*   ISBN: *1-59462-308-2*   **$13.45**
In these days of advanced thinking it is a matter of common observation that we have left many of the old landmarks behind and that we are now pressing forward to greater heights and to a wider horizon than that which represented the mind-content of our progenitors... Astrology Pages 144

Thought Vibration or The Law of Attraction in the Thought World   ISBN: *1-59462-127-6*   **$12.95**
by William Walker Atkinson   Psychology/Religion Pages 144

Optimism *by Helen Keller*   ISBN: *1-59462-108-X*   **$15.95**
Helen Keller was blind, deaf, and mute since 19 months old, yet famously learned how to overcome these handicaps, communicate with the world, and spread her lectures promoting optimism. An inspiring read for everyone... Biographies/Inspirational Pages 84

Sara Crewe *by Frances Burnett*   ISBN: *1-59462-360-0*   **$9.45**
In the first place, Miss Minchin lived in London. Her home was a large, dull, tall one, in a large, dull square, where all the houses were alike, and all the sparrows were alike, and where all the door-knockers made the same heavy sound... Childrens/Classic Pages 88

The Autobiography of Benjamin Franklin *by Benjamin Franklin*   ISBN: *1-59462-135-7*   **$24.95**
The Autobiography of Benjamin Franklin has probably been more extensively read than any other American historical work, and no other book of its kind has had such ups and downs of fortune. Franklin lived for many years in England, where he was agent... Biographies/History Pages 332

Name	
Email	
Telephone	
Address	
City, State ZIP	

☐ **Credit Card**   ☐ **Check / Money Order**

Credit Card Number	
Expiration Date	
Signature	

Please Mail to: Book Jungle
PO Box 2226
Champaign, IL 61825
or Fax to: 630-214-0564

ORDERING INFORMATION

web: *www.bookjungle.com*
email: *sales@bookjungle.com*
fax: *630-214-0564*
mail: *Book Jungle PO Box 2226 Champaign, IL 61825*
or PayPal *to sales@bookjungle.com*

Please contact us for bulk discounts

DIRECT-ORDER TERMS

**20% Discount if You Order
Two or More Books**
Free Domestic Shipping!
Accepted: Master Card, Visa,
Discover, American Express

www.ingramcontent.com/pod-product-compliance
Lightning Source LLC
Chambersburg PA
CBHW081306200626
46813CB00018B/3290